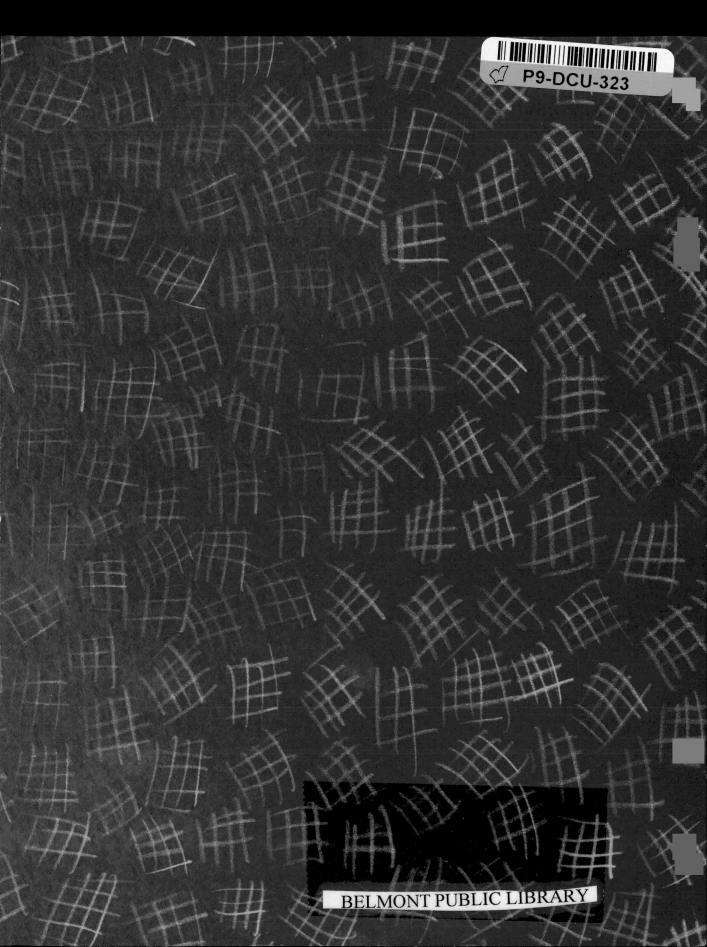

P9-DCU-323

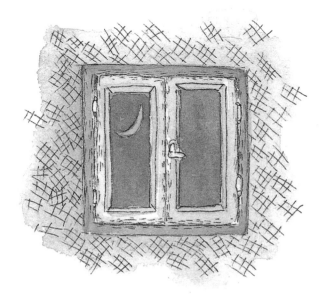

For Thomas

GOOD NIGHT SLEEP TIGHT

Eleven-and-a-half Good Night Stories
with Fox and Rabbit

Kristina Andres

Translated by Sally-Ann Spencer

GECKO PRESS

First Story

Fox and Rabbit lived quite far away, in a bright little house beyond the molehills.

One night Rabbit came racing home across the fields and up to the door, which Fox had locked because it was almost midnight. Inside, Fox was lying awake with a hollow feeling in his belly. He had been up three times already for something to eat. A bowl of pasta with sauce. Another bowl of pasta with sauce. Then a bowl of pasta without sauce, because the sauce was all gone. But the hollow feeling was still there.

When Rabbit knocked, Fox opened straightaway.

Rabbit was too out of puff to say a thing, so Fox went first.

"Rabbit, I can't sleep! There's a hole in my belly, as if something's missing!"

"I haven't said good night to you yet," panted Rabbit.

"That must be it!" said Fox.

"Good—night—Fox!" Rabbit puffed.

"Good night, Rabbit!

Fox sighed happily, slammed the door, sank back into bed, and fell fast asleep.

"Fox! You forgot to let me in!" Rabbit called through the door. But he didn't want to wake his friend, so he curled up on the doorstep and went to sleep.

When Fox got up the next morning he couldn't open the door.

"Huh, it's Rabbit. He must have forgotten to come inside, and now he's asleep on the doorstep."

Fox didn't want to wake his friend, but he needed to buy some things for breakfast. He didn't think of going through the window: he climbed up the chimney instead. Black from the tip of his snout to the tuft of his tail, he set out for the village.

The baker mistook him for the wolf in the leather jacket and
quickly gave him a cake before the wolf could threaten him.
 The butcher pressed a string of sausages into his paws.

And the grocer threw a cabbage at his head.

Fox was starting to have a funny feeling, so he ran straight home. He had all he could carry, anyway.

Back at the house, Rabbit had woken and come up with the idea of climbing in through the chimney. Inside he slipped into Fox's bed, which was still warm.

When Fox came in, there was no sign of Rabbit, but a black smudge was lying in his bed.

"No wonder they were giving me strange looks! I left my shadow at home."

He didn't want to wake his shadow, so he set the table very quietly.

Rabbit woke to the smell of cake—or was it cabbage? He got up and took his usual place at the table.

"Yikes!" yelped Fox when he turned and saw his shadow waiting quietly at the table.

"Yikes!" squeaked Rabbit when he saw the wolf in the leather jacket.

Then they gathered their wits.

"Fox?" said Rabbit.

"I thought you were my shadow," said Fox. "You're pitch-black, and everyone in the village was giving me strange looks."

"I expect they mistook you for the wolf in the leather jacket. You're pitch-black as well."

They racked their brains but couldn't think why they looked so different. In the end it was Rabbit who worked it out.

"It's night dust. It must have stuck to us because we went to sleep so late."

"We'd better go back to bed and sleep it off then," said Fox.

Worn out from all the sausages, cake and cabbage, they curled up under the covers just before lunchtime and slept until the next day.

In the morning they were still pitch-black.

Luckily Elephant came to visit and took them for a swim in the lake. And afterwards they looked just like Fox and Rabbit again. ☾

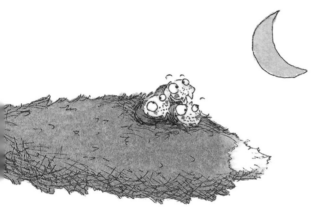

Second Story

"A very good night to you, dear Fox," Rabbit said solemnly.

"Dear Rabbit! A very good night to you too," replied Fox.

"To me *too*?" said Rabbit. "Who besides you wishes me good night?"

"I do!" sang the moon. "Good night to you, Rabbit. And good night to Fox as well."

"Good night," sighed the rose outside the window.

"Good night," the pear trees whispered.

"Good night! Good night! Good night!" piped the fleas on Fox's tail.

"Good night," the stars chimed.

"Good night," the raspberries murmured.

"Fox!" Rabbit's eyes were wide. "I think it's time we went to bed."

Third Story

One night there was a storm. Fox and Rabbit said good night and snuggled down under the warm covers. The wind rattled at the window.

"Do you think it wants to come in?" asked Fox.

"Maybe it wants to say good night," said Rabbit. "Does anyone ever wish the wind good night?"

Fox slid out of bed and opened the window. "Good night, wind!" he called.

At that, the wind rushed into the house, swept the apples off the table, hurled the kettle from the stove, blew open the wardrobe and tossed out some socks. It flung the covers from the bed, scattered ash around the room, roared back outside and shook the branches of the pear tree.

Then it was still.

"How about that!" Fox whispered happily in the dark. ☾

Fourth Story

In winter, when the wind whistled cold and relentless around the house, Fox and Rabbit went to bed early. One evening, Fox wanted to wish Rabbit an extra special good night.

"Listen, Rabbit! This is going to be amazing!" Then he began:
"Dear Rabbit, I wish you a good night with sweet dreams of
juicy carrots growing in a field, and a nice plump pear gleaming
in the sun that smells so good that butterflies come fluttering…
and a sponge cake! And liver sausage with lovely big lumps of
fat—but no onions! And honey-roasted goose with freshly laid

quail eggs. And chicken soup on the stove! And crispy little
tartlets with ham. And a huge steak with fried eggs on top.
And…worm salad with mayonnaise! And thick fish patties!
And goulash with a dash of cream…"

Fox fell asleep with a blissful sigh.

Rabbit stared at the wall. His eyes were wide open.

"Three rows of lettuce first thing, lush green grass, and buttercups that turn your teeth yellow…" he whispered. "Wild clover humming with bees, chive toast with yarrow flower and fleawort, and carrot cake and wobbly apple jelly, and beech tree bark… And an afternoon with Elephant, dozing beside the lake…"

And then at last, Rabbit fell asleep. ☾

Fifth Story

One night in summer Fox and Rabbit went down to the lake with Kangaroo. They caught three fat fish, then Kangaroo filled her pouch with water. They dropped the fish inside, where they darted to and fro and made Kangaroo laugh.

"That tickles!"

Most of the water had already sloshed out.

"How are we going to get the fish home?" said Fox. "They're too restless. They need to go to sleep."

"I'll say good night, so they know what to do," said Rabbit. He peered into Kangaroo's pouch and said in a solemn voice: "Good night!" Then: "Sleep tight!"

Kangaroo couldn't stop laughing.

Fox had a go: "Goood niigght!"

The fish didn't look very tired.

"Kangaroo, why don't you walk around slowly. That might calm them down," said Fox.

Kangaroo walked in a slow circle. It wasn't easy because kangaroos prefer to hop. "They slow down when I'm near the water, but they start tickling again as soon as I move away."

"Maybe you should stand in the lake," said Rabbit. "Then they're bound to go to sleep."

Kangaroo waded out to her knees.

Plop! Plop! Plop! The fish flipped into the lake…

"Now we know that fish aren't silly!" said Kangaroo, recovering from the shock. "And I need a lie-down—on dry land!" ☾

Sixth Story

Elephant had told them that he always counted sheep to send himself to sleep.

"Sheep make my whiskers stand on end," said Fox. "Think what would happen if I had to count them! I'd never get to sleep."

"Sheep eat all the tastiest flowers in the field," said Rabbit. "There's no way I'm going to count them!"

"If we're going to count anything, we should count good nights. Then at least we won't forget why we're doing it."

"Good idea! Shall we try it, Fox?"

They turned off the light and went to bed.

Rabbit started. "One good night, two good nights, three good nights, four good nights, five good nights…"

Fox took over. Then Rabbit went on. They counted and counted. After an hour of good nights, they were bored with counting in the dark so they turned on the light. For every good night, they bounced on the bed. Then they tried jumping from the wardrobe onto the mattress. It was fun for a while, but soon they needed something new.

"Five-hundred-and-thirty-four good nights!" counted Fox. He did a handstand on the kitchen table, grabbed hold of the light, and landed—hooray!—on the wardrobe before leaping onto the bed.

"Five-hundred-and-thirty-five good nights!" counted
Rabbit as he launched himself off the bed, crossed the floor
in a somersault, climbed backwards up the table leg, did a
handstand, grabbed hold of the light, and landed—hooray!
—on the wardrobe before springing onto the bed.

Outside, the crescent moon crossed the sky and faded from view. The sun climbed over the hills and poured in through the window. It shone on a cloudburst of feathers strewn about the house. It shone on Fox who had fallen asleep on top of the wardrobe and on Rabbit who was snoring under the table.

Outside, a flock of sheep bustled past.

"Baa! Baa! Baa!"

Fox groaned. "I was asleep already! Try Elephant—in the blue house to the left!" ☾

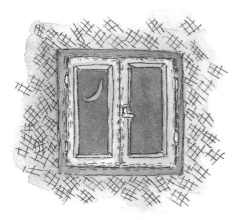

Seventh Story

"Every night we say the same old good night," Fox complained.

Rabbit had a think. "What if we say it with different words for 'good' and 'night'?"

Fox agreed to try, and he thought of something at once: "I wish you a happy new darkness!"

"And I wish you a merry dusk!" said Rabbit straight back.

Fox wished Rabbit a splendid blackness.

Then Rabbit wished Fox soothing dark.

"Soft shadows, Rabbit!"

"Magnificent moonlight, Fox!"

Then they were silent for a while.

"It's not the same as saying good night," said Fox. "Good night, Rabbit!"

Rabbit sighed happily. "Good night, Fox!" ☾

Eighth Story

One night in summer Fox and Rabbit set off on an adventure. They packed three rounds of cheese, a frying pan and their tent. Then they walked to the top of the hill. They had just started frying the cheese when Elephant came along.

"Can I have some too?"

Elephant ate three cheeses.

The tent door was open. It looked snug inside.

"Can I sleep here too?"

"All right," said Fox. "But only if Rabbit sleeps in the middle."

They lay with their heads near the door so they could stare into the night. Elephant's side of the tent made a great bulge.

The grassy slopes were dotted with sleeping sheep that looked like boulders.

Elephant couldn't get to sleep. "One sheep, two sheep, three sheep…" he counted.

Rabbit glanced at Fox. "Counting makes me tired in the morning," he whispered. "Last time I was sore all over."

"Me too," whispered Fox.

After a while the fire went out and the night became pitch-black. At the bottom of the hill something glinted. Elephant stopped counting. "Look! A star! It's coming to join us."

But it wasn't a star blinking in the dark as it came ever closer: it was Granny Wolf's gold tooth. Granny Wolf was dangerous because she liked to swing her old black umbrella at anyone in reach.

"Granny Wolf is scary," Elephant whispered. "I don't like the way she growls."

But that night Granny Wolf was very quiet. She sneaked up silently on the sheep, and not to wish them good night.

Rabbit, Fox and Elephant held their breath and lay very still. Granny Wolf was so close they could smell her old wool dress.

Suddenly there was a commotion. Granny Wolf tripped over a tent peg and kicked the frying pan. It clattered down the hillside and landed among the sheep. Granny Wolf howled curses and swung her umbrella. But it was too dark for anyone to see.

All at once, Lottie the big sheepdog appeared outside the tent.
She shone her light straight at Granny Wolf's gold tooth.

"Go home, Granny Wolf, or there'll be trouble!" she said
firmly.

She reached into her backpack and handed Granny a sandwich. Granny Wolf trundled off without a word. She knew better than to argue with Lottie.

"All right, my lovelies," said Lottie. "I have sandwiches for you too. Eat up—then sleep tight!" She waved her cap and hurried off to find her scattered flock.

Fox, Rabbit and Elephant gobbled up their sandwiches, then fell straight to sleep. The night was filled with smells of wool and grassy burps. Stars twinkled in the sky. Outside the tent, Lottie kept watch. And from inside came sheepy snores. ☽

Eighth Story (and a Half)

"When you wish someone good night," said Rabbit, "you have to do it quietly and carefully. Otherwise the wish won't work." He picked up an apple that was half red and half green. He turned the red side towards him and whispered: "Good night, dear one."

The apple was silent.

Rabbit bit into the red side and gave the rest to Fox.

Fox took a bite of the green side and made a face. "Yuck!"

He tossed the apple out of the window. It sailed through the pitch-black night and glanced off the snout of the wolf in the leather jacket who was scrumping pears from their tree.

"Hey!" said the wolf in the leather jacket. "I'll be coming for you next!"

Rabbit slammed the window shut. "Did you have to do that, Fox? He's angry now!"

"He's always angry!" muttered Fox.

Because they needed a treat after that, Rabbit made semolina pudding with sweet raspberries. They went to bed feeling warm and full.

"Good night," they whispered.

Only the wolf in the leather jacket was wide awake.
He had to stew the pears now: he was making his
grandmother's breakfast. ☾

Ninth Story

One night Fox slept like a log. It made him and Rabbit wonder what else they could sleep like. They decided to try something out with Kangaroo and Elephant.

"Tonight we're not going to sleep like Fox, Rabbit, Kangaroo or Elephant. We're going to sleep like something else!" Rabbit announced.

They waited until dark, then it was time to decide what.

They let Elephant choose.

"We'll sleep like bats," he declared. "Upside down."

"Bats don't sleep any old where," said Fox. "They find exactly the right place to roost."

So they had to find the right place.

The attic? It was dusty and full of clutter. There were upturned chairs, paintbrushes and other things that could poke them in the eye.

"How about the garden?" said Rabbit.

The night was warm and dry, so the others agreed.

They stood outside.

"Where, do you think?" asked Kangaroo.

"In the pear tree!" said Elephant.

The pear tree rustled nervously, but none of them heard.

Fox climbed up first, then Rabbit, then Kangaroo. Elephant went last. The pear tree groaned. They each chose a branch, hooked their legs around it, and dangled upside down.

There was a strange fluttering nearby.

"What's that?" said Elephant. "Not gnats?"

"It's them!" Rabbit whispered dramatically. "The bats!"

"Why aren't they sleeping?" asked Kangaroo.

"They're watching," said Fox. "To see how it's done."

He raised his voice. "Hello, bats! You can copy us if you like!"

They shut their eyes and tried to sleep while the bats rustled between the branches.

"My eyelids keep opening," grumbled Kangaroo. "They won't stay closed."

"Same here," muttered Rabbit.

"It's because we're upside down," said Fox. "How are we supposed to sleep if our eyelids keep falling open?" He sounded cross.

Elephant sighed. It was the same for him. "Maybe we should sleep like pears instead. It'll be much easier and we can stay where we are."

The pear tree had other plans. It was a strong, kind tree, but it couldn't carry such enormous pears. There was a great rustling as it gave itself a shake, then came three small thumps and a gigantic thud. They were down.

The bats wheeled about over the little garden. Perhaps they had been watching closely.

"What a dreadful way to sleep," said Fox with feeling. "Good night, bats! And good luck!" ☾

Tenth Story

Fox and Rabbit had won a new clock in a raffle. A shiny clock with ticking hands. They hung it on the wall.

Now they always knew when it was time for breakfast, lunch, afternoon tea and dinner. They even knew when it was time to say good night.

At eight o'clock they wished each other good night for the first time. At quarter past eight they wished each other good night for the second time. At half past eight for the third time. And so on.

At midnight they were still awake.

"I can't sleep," grumbled Fox.

"And soon it'll be time to get up," groaned Rabbit.

It went on like that for weeks. They had never felt so dreadful.

One night Fox forgot to close the front door.

The moon shone into the house. The clock gleamed on the wall. And in the doorway gleamed a gold tooth.

"Keep perfectly still," Fox hissed in Rabbit's ear.

Rabbit didn't want a visit from Granny Wolf. No one ever wanted a visit from Granny Wolf. No one with any sense would let her in. Had the clock made Fox lose his mind?

There was a clunk. The gold gleam disappeared.

Fox waited until he was sure that Granny Wolf had really left. Then he got up, locked the door, and turned on the light.

He yelped with joy. Granny Wolf had stolen the clock.

Rabbit sank with relief back onto his pillow. "I'm so happy, Fox," he said. "Good night."

"I'm happy too, Rabbit. Good night."

And they fell asleep. They slept deeply and silently, like a hundred logs. They had all the time in the world.

Back in her house, Granny Wolf sat in bed and clasped the clock in her paws. Her eyes gleamed. She was much too happy to go to sleep. ☾

Eleventh Story

Rabbit had a cough and didn't feel well, so Fox was writing
a good night book. He wrote down all the things that had
happened to them both. Then he sat on the bed and read aloud
to Rabbit.

He read about the night dust that had clung to them, and
about the time the raspberries wished them good night. He read
about saying good night without saying "good" and "night",
and about the restless fish in Kangaroo's pouch. About how the
wind came in through the window, and how they counted good
nights. About camping on the hill, and sleeping like bats, and
about the clock that kept them awake all night.

Fox read and read until it was dark. Then he opened the window to let in some air. The cherry tree had blossomed, and earlier that day bees had visited to tell the flowers about the tasty red cherries that would come. Now a gust of wind swept the tired petals from the tree and through the window into the house. More and more of them.

"Snow! Let's go sledding, Fox," Rabbit mumbled in his fever.

Fox fetched the sled and lifted Rabbit onto it. He tucked him in snugly and pulled a pompom hat over his ears. He pushed the sled back and forth through the petals, for minutes then for hours. Rabbit sang deliriously about snow and sheep and all the white things he could think of, until finally he fell asleep.

Fox scribbled down the story about sledding through cherry blossoms, then he dozed off too.

In the morning, Rabbit woke up feeling fresh and strong.
He picked up Fox's book and read it from start to finish.
Then he added some pictures because Fox hadn't drawn any.
And he came up with a title:

Good Night, Sleep Tight
Eleven-and-a-half Good Night Stories
with Fox and Rabbit

To finish off, he wrote on the wall above the bed—very quietly
because he didn't want to wake anyone:

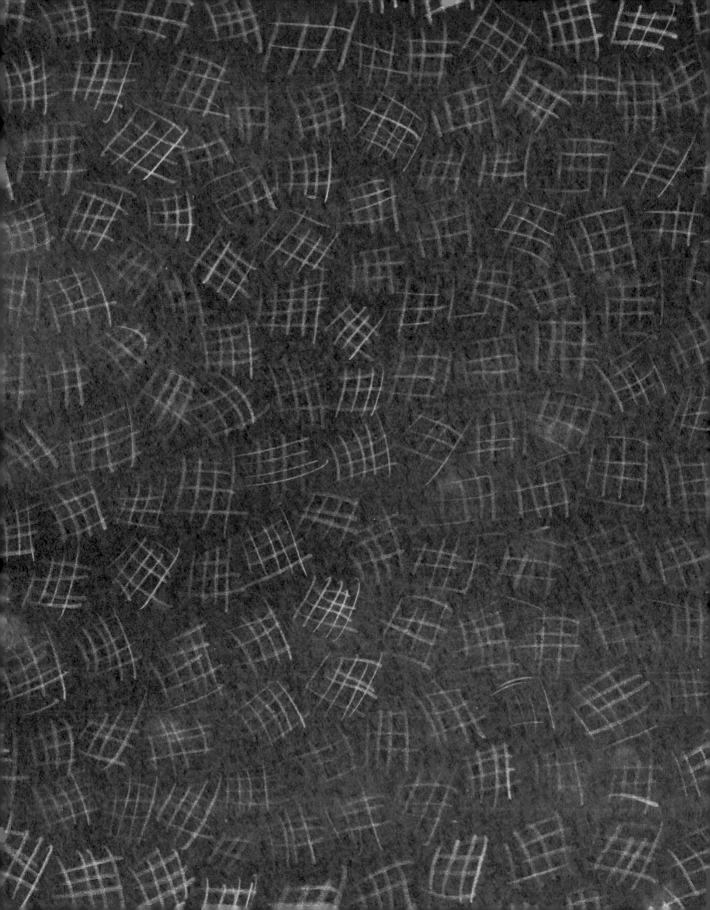

First American edition published 2018 by Gecko
Press USA, an imprint of Gecko Press Ltd.

This edition first published in 2017
by Gecko Press
PO Box 9335, Wellington 6141, New Zealand
info@geckopress.com

English language edition
© Gecko Press Ltd 2017
Translation © Sally-Ann Spencer 2017

ISBN: 978-1-776571-43-7

Text and illustrations: Kristina Andres
Title of the original edition: *Nun schlaft mal
schön! Elfeinhalb Gutenachtgeschichten von
Fuchs und Hase*
© 2016 Moritz Verlag, Frankfurt am Main
English language edition arranged through
Mundt Agency, Düsseldorf

Distributed in the United States and Canada by
Lerner Publishing Group, lernerbooks.com
Distributed in the United Kingdom by Bounce
Sales and Marketing, bouncemarketing.co.uk
Distributed in Australia by Scholastic
Australia, scholastic.com.au
Distributed in New Zealand by Upstart
Distribution, upstartpress.co.nz

The translation of this book was supported by a
grant from the Goethe-Institut which is funded
by the German Ministry of Foreign Affairs.

GOETHE
INSTITUT

Edited by Penelope Todd
Design and typesetting by Sarah Maxey
Printed in China by Everbest Printing
Co Ltd, an accredited ISO 14001 & FSC
certified printer

**For more curiously good books,
visit geckopress.com**